TEN LiTTLE FLAKEY TURTLES

CORRiE HARRiS AND DEBRA HARRiS

ARCHWAY PUBLISHING BOOKS MAY BE ORDERED THROUGH BOOKSELLERS OR BY CONTACTING:

ARCHWAY PUBLISHING
1663 LIBERTY DRIVE
BLOOMINGTON, IN 47403
WWW.ARCHWAYPUBLISHING.COM
844-669-3957

ISBN: 978-1-6657-0297-3 (SC)
ISBN: 978-1-6657-0298-0 (HC)
ISBN: 978-1-6657-0296-6 (E)

PRINT INFORMATION AVAILABLE ON THE LAST PAGE.

ARCHWAY PUBLISHING REV. DATE: 05/14/2021

END OF SCHOOL, WE ARE GOING ON VACATION ON THE BEACH.
I LOVE THE BEACH. WE ARE GOING TO MY GRANDFATHER'S
BEACH HOUSE DOWN BY THE SEASHORE WHERE HE STUDIED
ENDANGERED SPECIES.

THE BEACH HOUSE WAS JUST LIKE IN A MOVIE. IT WAS A STRAW LIKE HUT. I HAD MY OWN ROOM, WITH A DOOR THAT OPENS TO THE BEACH.

PREPARING FOR BED I COULD NOT WAIT, TO GO COLLECT SEASHELL, BUILD SANDCASTLES ON THE BEACH IN THE SUN. THERE WAS A LITTLE BLUE NIGHT LIGHT, SO I TURNED IT ON IN THE ROOM, IT BEGAN TO FEEL WARM AND DREAMY.

I DRIFTED OFF TO SLEEP. THEN I THOUGHT I WAS DREAMING THERE WERE THESE FLAKEY LITTLE ANIMALS CRAWLING AROUND MY FLOOR. THEY LOOKED LIKE A PIECE OF MOVING CARPET, BUT INSTEAD LITTLE TURTLES ALL GROUPED TOGETHER!

I MOVED TO THE SIDE OF THE BED AND REACHED DOWN TO TOUCH ONE.

HIS SHELL WAS COVERED WITH SOFT FLAKES! THEN I FELL ASLEEP. WHEN MORNING CAME, I THOUGHT IT WAS A DREAM. BUT WHEN I TURNED, THEY WERE ALL ON MY BED WITH LOTS OF QUESTIONS.

ONE TURTLE LOOKED UP AT ME AND SAID, "HI! YOU ARE NOT THE LITTLE GIRL FROM LAST YEAR. WE SAW THE BLUE LIGHT, THAT IS WHY WE CAME. SHE WAS OUR FRIEND, BUT SHE COULD NOT TAKE US HOME WITH HER."

HE WAS A SMALL FLAKEY TURTLE WITH A HOOK BREAK. AND HE HAD THE PRETTIEST, BIG BLUE EYE AND A HAPPY LITTLE VOICE.

I SAID, "YOU TALK!"
HE REPLIED, "ONLY TO SPECIAL PEOPLE, NOT TO EVERYONE."

WHAT IS YOUR NAME? WHERE DID YOU COME FROM?

"PENNY STAMPS."

SHE SAID, "NEW YORK CITY."

WHO ARE YOU?

"I'M BINKIE."

MY MOTHER CALLS ME TO EAT, THEN SUDDENLY THEY DISAPPEARED. WHERE DID THEY GO?

I TOLD MY PARENTS, THEY SAID I WAS DREAMING THERE IS NO TALKING TURTLES OR FLAKEY TURTLES, BUT I WAS AWAKE WHEN I SAW THEM.

BACK IN MY ROOM, THEY FOLLOWED ME ALL AROUND,
WATCHING EVERYTHING I DID.

THE SUN WAS HOT, SO I TOOK AN UMBRELLA, MY BUCKET, AND TOWEL. I WAS GOING TO BUILD THE BIGGEST SANDCASTLE EVER TODAY. IT WILL HAVE EIGHT ROOMS. WHEN I STARTED WORKING, THERE WAS ONE TURTLE, THEN ANOTHER TURTLE. THEY WERE MOVING IN AND OUT OF THE ROOMS IN MY CASTLE. THEY SAID "WILL THIS BE OUR HOUSE?

"IF YOU WANT IT TO BE," I SAID. THEY WERE SMALL ENOUGH TO LIVE IN IT.

"HERE COMES MY DAD. HE WILL LIKE YOU."

DAD LOOKED AROUND, WHAT TURTLES? THEIR GONE! DAD AND I SAT AND WATCH THE WATER. I CANNOT UNDERSTAND HOW THEY GOT AWAY SO FAST. MAYBE THEY ARE IN THE CASTLE. NO NOT THERE. MAYBE THEY ARE MAGICAL AND CAN DISAPPEAR WHEN THEY WANT TO.

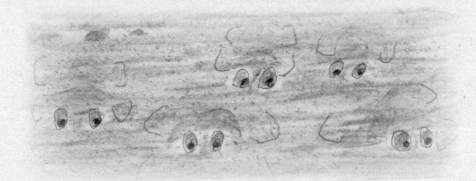

WHEN DAD WENT INSIDE THE TURTLES REAPPEARED. WHY DID YOU HIDE? AND WHERE DID YOU GO?

ONE TURTLE SAID, "WE WERE HERE ALL THE TIME. BUT HIDING IN THE SAND. WE WERE AFRAID, ADULTS TOOK OUR PARENTS AND WE NEVER SAW THEM AGAIN. WE WAITED NEAR THE HOUSE HOPING THEY WOULD COME BACK. WE MEET LOTS OF CHILDREN, BUT THEY DO NOT TAKE US HOME AS PETS."

WE PLAYED IN THE SAND AND THEY CRAWLED UP MY LEGS AND STARED AT MY TOES. I CLIMBED TO MY FEET. IT MADE ME LAUGH BECAUSE THEY FELT FUNNY ON MY SKIN. I HELD ONE IN MY HAND, THEY ARE SO CUTE AND TINY. I HAVE NEVER SEEN TURTLES LIKE THESE BEFORE. THEY CRAWLED ON MY HAND, BACK AND, EVEN ON TOP OF MY HEAD. EVERY DAY WE PLAYED ON THE BEACH. ON RAINY DAYS WE PLAYED IN MY ROOM.

THE TURTLES TRAVELED WITH ME IN MY POCKETBOOK AND POCKET.

I SHOWED THEM BOOKS AND TALKED TO THEM ABOUT THE MANY THINGS I DO AT HOME. AND EXPLAIN WHAT SCHOOL IS. THEN ONE SAID, "MY MOTHER HAD SCHOOL SHE WOULD TEACH US HOW TO HIDE, HUNT, AND WHAT WERE THE RIGHT THINGS TO EAT AND WHAT WERE NOT. SHE TAUGHT US WHERE IT IS DANGEROUS FOR US TO GO NOW. WE MUST REMEMBER BECAUSE SHE IS GONE."

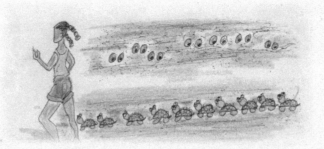

WE SWAM IN THE CLEAR BLUE WATER. THEY FOLLOWED ME ON THE BEACH LIKE I WAS THE MOTHER TURTLE if ANYONE CAME CLOSE, THEY WOULD HiDE IN THE SAND.

"YOU WiLL GO HOME WiTH ME WE WiLL GET THROUGH THiS WHOLE DAY, BEFORE I GO HOME, YOU WiLL SEE. MY PARENTS WiLL LET ME HAVE ALL OF YOU AS PETS YOU ARE SMALL AND DO NOT EAT MUCH AND I CAN MAKE A LiTTLE PLACE iN MY ROOM."

I LET THEM LEAP iN MY BED AND RiDE iN MY POCKETS, THEY BROUGHT ME BEAUTIFUL BRiGHT-COLORED SEASHELLS. THEY HELPED ME COLLECT SEASHELL. AND WE RESTED UNDER THE UMBRELLA.

"WiLL YOU TAKE US HOME AS YOUR PETS?" A TURTLE ASKED.

"IF MY PARENTS SAY iT iS OK, I SAID.

"PARENTS DO NOT LiKE US. THEY NEVER LET THE BOYS AND GiRLS TAKE US HOME." "WHY?" I ASKED.

"I DO NOT KNOW," HE SAiD

THE LAST DAY OF VACATION WAS COMING SOON.
I ASKED MY MOTHER IF I COULD HAVE A PET.
SHE SAID, "YES. WHAT DID I HAVE IN MIND?"
"WELL, COULD I HAVE MORE THAN ONE?" I ASKED.

SHE SAID, "OK". THEY WERE JUMPING UP AND DOWN IN MY POCKET WITH JOY. ON HER WAY OUT THE ROOM, SHE SAID, WHAT KIND OF PETS?

I SAID, "TURTLES."

SHE SAID, "OK."

THEN I SAID, "TEN."

SHE CAME BACK, "TEN? WHERE WILL YOU PUT TEN TURTLES IN YOUR ROOM?

I SAID, "THEY ARE VERY SMALL."

"I NEED TO TALK WITH YOUR FATHER TO SEE WHAT HE HAS TO SAY," SHE ANSWERED.

WE WERE PLAYING ON THE BEACH WHEN MY PARENT CAME OUT. MOM SAID, "YOUR DAD KNOWS A LITTLE ABOUT TURTLES. HIS FATHER STUDIED THEM YEARS AGO. I NEED TO SEE WHAT KIND OF TURTLES THEY ARE."

PENNY REACHED IN HER POCKET AND TOOK SOME OUT IN HER HAND AND SHOWED THEM TO HER FATHER.

HER DAD SAID, THESE TURTLES ARE RARE, AND YOU ONLY SEE THEM EVERY TWENTY YEARS, IF THEY LIVE OR POACHERS DO NOT STEAL THEM. YOU THINK I COULD SEE THEM?

I SAID, "YOU ALL COME OUT AND SAY HELLO."

THEY PEEPED UP FROM THE SAND AND ALL SAID, "HELLO. HELLO. HELLO."

DAD SAID, "TURTLES DO NOT TALK."

I LAUGHED SO LOUD. "IT IS A SOUND THAT THEY MAKE FROM THERE THROAT."

MY PARENTS STARTED LAUGHING AND THEN THEY ALL CAME OUT. MOTHER SAID, "THEY'RE BEAUTIFUL!"

AND FATHER WAS JUST ASTONISHED AT HOW THEY LOOKED AND FELT. HE SAID, "MY FATHER STUDIED AND RESEARCHED THE LITTLE GUYS FOR YEARS. NOW HERE I AM HOLDING TEN FLAKEY TURTLES. WE CANNOT KEEP THEM AS PETS. THEY ARE RARE AND ENDANGER SPECIES. THE GOVERNMENT WILL ESTABLISH A PROTECTIVE HABITAT FOR THEM. THEIR PARENTS WERE PROBABLY STOLEN. THEY ARE EXPENSIVE.

DAD WENT ON, "WE NEED TO CONTACT A GOVERNMENT AGENCY TO ESTABLISH A PROTECTIVE HABITAT.

THEY WILL ESTABLISH A PROTECTIVE AREA TO STUDY AND CARE FOR THEM. BUT THEY WILL NOT BE PETS. WITH THIS GROUP, WE CAN BRING BACK THEIR SPECIES. THEY WILL BE IN AN AREA WHERE CHILDREN CAN COME SEE THEM AND PEOPLE WILL BE THERE TO STUDY AND CARE FOR THEM. THEY WILL BE PETS FOR MANY PEOPLE AND WE WILL COME BACK TO SEE THEM EVERY YEAR."

I ASKED THE TURTLES IS THAT OK WITH YOU ALL?
BINKIE SAID, (COULD WE KEEP THE BLUE LIGHT.)
PENNY REPLIED, (YES.)

AS DAD WAVED GOODBYE, I COULD SEE THEM PEEPING UP OUT OF HIS POCKET.

THE GOVERNMENT ESTABLISHED A PROTECTIVE AREA FOR THE TURTLES CALL THE BLUE LIGHT HABITAT. MY FATHER STAYED BEHIND TO HELP SET UP THE HABITAT BECAUSE IT WAS SOMETHING HIS FATHER WOULD REALLY WANT. DAD THINKS THEY CANNOT TALK, BUT THEY TALK TO ME. I AM SURE IN TIME THEY WILL TALK TO HIM.

Printed in the United States
by Baker & Taylor Publisher Services